G K Chesterton was born in London in 1874 and was educated at St Paul's School. He became a journalist and began writing for *The Speaker* with his friend Hilaire Belloc. His first novel, *The Napoleon of Notting Hill,* was published in 1904. In this book Chesterton developed his political attitudes in which he attacked socialism, big business and technology and showed how they become the enemies of freedom and justice. These were themes which were to run through his other works.

Chesterton converted to Catholicism in 1922. He explored his belief in his many religious essays and books. The best known is *Orthodoxy,* his personal spiritual odyssey.

His output was prolific. He wrote a great variety of books from biographies on Shaw and Dickens to literary criticism. He also produced poetry and many volumes of political, social and religious essays. His style is marked by vigour, puns, paradoxes and a great intelligence and personal modesty.

Chesterton is perhaps best known for his Father Brown stories. Father Brown is a modest Catholic priest who uses careful psychology to put himself in the place of the criminal in order to solve the crime.

Chesterton died in 1936.

BY THE SAME AUTHOR
ALL PUBLISHED BY HOUSE OF STRATUS

GENERAL FICTION:
THE BALL AND THE CROSS
THE MAN WHO KNEW TOO MUCH
THE NAPOLEON OF NOTTING HILL
THE PARADOXES OF MR POND
THE POET AND THE LUNATICS
THE RETURN OF DON QUIXOTE

BIOGRAPHY:
CHARLES DICKENS
CHAUCER
GEORGE BERNARD SHAW
ROBERT BROWNING
ROBERT LOUIS STEVENSON
WILLIAM BLAKE

G K CHESTERTON

Wine, Water and Song

WITH AN INTRODUCTION BY L. A. G. STRONG

This edition published in 2008 by House of Stratus, an imprint of
Stratus Books Ltd., 21 Beeching Park, Kelly Bray,
Cornwall, PL17 8QS, UK.

www.houseofstratus.com

Typeset, printed and bound by House of Stratus.

A catalogue record for this book is available from the British Library.

ISBN 07551-165-4-2

Contents

INTRODUCTION

The British public likes its writers to be consistent. When it thinks of them at all, it wants to know what to think. It requires a label, a pigeon-hole. It needs to feel sure that Miss A's latest book will contain the mixture as before, and that Mr B's will once again expound the views that made his name.

This foible, while often soothing to Miss A and to Mr B brings disadvantages. As long as the mixture and the views remain popular, all is well. But, should tastes change, Mr B and Miss A may find their labels turned to millstones. Even though they too have moved with the times, the utmost sincerity or adroitness may fail to free them from their accepted labels and persuade the British public to attach new ones.

Things are even worse if the original labels touch controversial matters; as in the case of G K Chesterton. Chesterton suffered from the start under our national love of labels. He had a very large following, as his publishers have good reason to know: but, in view of his tremendous gifts and his essentially English character, there were too many whom he might have called abstainers. Lately, his reputation has been in decline. Great numbers of potential readers are put off by a label which, from being a millstone, has come dangerously near to being a gravestone. They picture an obese and hearty figure banging a pewter pot upon a table and bellowing a paean in praise of beer and the Pope: and they abstain.

The picture is unjust, and wrongs a writer of vigorous, noble, and tender imagination. But for his Church, Chesterton would have been a pagan. He avows it, in deriding Mr Mandragon, the Millionaire, who did not know how to live, and was cremated: –

> *And he lies there fluffy and soft and grey*
> *and certainly quite refined,*
> *When he might have rotted to flowers and fruit*
> *with Adam and all mankind,*
> *Or been eaten by wolves athirst for blood,*
> *Or burnt on a good tall pyre of wood*
> *In a towering flame, as a heathen should,*
> *Or even sat with us here at food...*

Even more explicit is the Song of the Strange Ascetic: –

> *If I had been a Heathen,*
> *I'd have praised the purple vine,*
> *My slaves should dig the vineyards*
> *And I would drink the wine...*

> *If I had been a Heathen,*
> *I'd have crowned Neœsra's curls,*
> *And filled my life with love affairs,*
> *My house with dancing girls...*

And he goes on to jeer at the "poor old sinner" who "sins without delight"; and, in conclusion, declares himself unable to read the riddle

> *Of them that do not have the faith,*
> *And will not have the fun.*

It would be fun, clearly; but Chesterton had the faith. He turned therefore to the celebration of those bodily pleasures on which the Church looked with tolerance: not the dancing girls, but eating and drinking. Claiming as his authority the miracle at the marriage feast at Cana in Galilee, he sang the praise of wine. A believer expresses his faith in the right use of the body, and the body thrives upon the right food and the right drink. Hurrah, then, for wine, for twopenny ale, for good red meat, for bacon and for pork: and be damned to vegetarian dishes, teetotallers, and every form of substitute and womanish victual and tipple.

> *For the wicked old women who feel well-bred*
> *Have turned to a tea-shop "The Saracen's Head."*

Yes, and worse.

> *Tea, although an Oriental,*
> *Is a gentleman at least;*
> *Cocoa is a cad and coward,*
> *Cocoa is a vulgar beast,*
> *Cocoa is a dull, disloyal,*
> *Lying, crawling cad and clown,*
> *And may very well be grateful,*
> *To the fool that takes him down.*
>
> *As for all the windy waters,*
> *They were rained like tempests down*
> *When good drink had been dishonoured*
> *By the tipplers of the town;*
> *When red wine had brought red ruin,*
> *And the death-dance of our times,*
> *Heaven sent us Soda Water*
> *As a torment for our crimes.*

I would like to have been by when someone offered him sherbet.

One of the difficulties about Chesterton was that he joked when he was in dead earnest. These quips and quiddities sprang from his deep ferocious faith. The average Englishman, who is not sure enough of his beliefs to jest about them, is apt to be embarrassed and put off Chesterton by what seems to him a lack of proportion. More than most writers, Chesterton was all of a piece. His imagination worked on many levels, from profound to trivial, but it was dominated always by the same enormous Facts. He would have said, it needed their discipline, for it was a strong, violent, gambolling imagination, disporting itself often in the meads of fancy, but leaping sometimes to summits – or depths – where few have the stomach to follow it.

One should not build too much on these songs, which are incidental to a prose fantasia, *The Flying Inn*, and have the colour of their context. Chesterton's deepest simplicity is not to be found in them, nor the clarity of vision in which, a terrible child, he glances back to Blake and to Swift. He is in lighter mood here, but he tells us what he believes, and he believes what he tells us.

> *My friends, we will not go again or ape an ancient rage,*
> *Or stretch the folly of our youth to be the shame of age,*
> *But walk with clearer eyes and ears this path that wandereth,*
> *And see undrugged in evening light the decent inn of death;*
> *For there is good news yet to hear and fine things to be seen,*
> *Before we go to Paradise by way of Kensal Green.*

There is more than rhetoric here; the fourth line is memorable. Do you notice, by the way, the double parallel to Dr Johnson, in "undrugged" and all the praise of inns with which the book is filled? Dr Johnson, who refused opiates at the last because they would cloud his faculties, and who said "There is no private house in which people can enjoy themselves so well, as at a capital tavern"? The two men had more in common than bulk and gusto. They had awe, fear of sin, loud laughter, and great kindness. The Doctor's voice was the deeper, but Chesterton would not have so condemned the unfortunate lady whom Boswell sought to excuse – "The woman's a whore, and there's an end on't."

> *Great Collingwood walked down the glade*
> *And flung the acorns free,*
> *That oaks might still be in the grove*

As oaken as the beams above,
When the great Lover sailors love
Was kissed by Death at sea…

Each had a deep tenderness, but Chesterton's charity could open wider arms.

This does not mean that there was anything blurred or sentimental in his views on human conduct. He had what many moralists lack, a vision of evil, too appalling to admit of compromise. Few men's work can shudder as can Chesterton's. This awareness of evil as a force in the universe was quite distinct from the small strain of morbidity which was one of his weaknesses, and betrayed him now and then into a female note of hysteria (I use the adjective not in sex prejudice, but because no other will express the incongruity in this male and roistering literary character). It was the note of fear, shrill in Walpole, sullen in Belloc, camouflaged in Maugham. Kipling blustered at his fear, Joyce shivered, Yeats raged; Virginia Woolf faced it; it made Chesterton querulous. All of them knew it: it was endemic in their time. Chesterton was fortified against it by his faith.

On the technical side he was, like most writers of fertile imagination, an admirer of Dickens – an influence as strong, and as dangerous, as that of Dr Johnson. A Dickensian exuberance, the consolations of faith, and a clear-cut moral judgment on first principles were none of them aids to popular esteem in the late interval between two wars. An added drawback to appreciation of his powers as poet was that Chesterton used the rhythms which the public had learned to associate with Kipling. If Chesterton was the truer poet, Kipling used them with unmatched brilliance and assurance: and the general reader, no stickler for niceties but no sort of a fool, decided that Chesterton was following the more famous writer, and at some distance. I am not maintaining for an instant that this is relevant to any proper consideration of Chesterton's merits, but it has gone to make a label, which is another name for a prejudice, and it is against prejudice that Chesterton's reputation has to fight today. He has, as I said before, a legion of admirers: but he would have two, three, four legions, if the old label could be removed, and new readers could be brought to look at him as he really is. Perhaps the reprinting of these verses may be a first step towards persuading them. I hope so. Those who love good writing care nothing about the swing of fashion and the ups and downs of reputation, but some may confess to a touch of partisanship: and, in any case, it would be fitting that a Christian writer of genius, who kicked hard on the backside all who would make Christianity prim and joyless, should have from a new generation of readers the welcome which his gifts deserve.

L A G STRONG

THE ENGLISHMAN

St George he was for England,
And before he killed the dragon
He drank a pint of English ale
Out of an English flagon.
For thought he fast right readily
In hair-shirt or in mail,
It isn't safe to give him cakes
Unless you give him ale.

St George he was for England,
And right gallantly set free
The lady left for dragon's meat
And tied up to a tree;
But since he stood for England
And knew what England means,
Unless you give him bacon
You mustn't give him beans.

St George he is for England,
And shall wear the shield he wore
When we go out in armour
With the battle-cross before.

1

But though he is jolly company
And very pleased to dine,
It isn't safe to give him nuts
Unless you give him wine.

WINE AND WATER

Old Noah he had an ostrich farm and
    fowls on the largest scale,
He ate his egg with a ladle in an egg-cup
    big as a pail,
And the soup he took was Elephant Soup
    and the fish he took was Whale,
But they all were small to the cellar he
    took when he set out to sail,
And Noah he often said to his wife when
    he sat down to dine,
"I don't care where the water goes if it
    doesn't get into the wine."

The cataract of the cliff of heaven fell
    blinding off the brink
As if it would wash the stars away as suds
    go down a sink,
The seven heavens came roaring down for
    the throats of hell to drink,
And Noah he cocked his eye and said,
    "It looks like rain, I think,
The water has drowned the Matterhorn
    as deep as a Mendip mine,
But I don't care where the water goes if

3

it doesn't get into the wine."

But Noah he sinned, and we have sinned;
on tipsy feet we trod,
Till a great big black teetotaller was sent
to us for a rod,
And you can't get wine at a P.S.A., or
chapel, or Eisteddfod,
For the Curse of Water has come again
because of the wrath of God,
And water is on the Bishop's board and
the Higher Thinker's shrine,
But I don't care where the water goes if
it doesn't get into the wine.

THE SONG AGAINST GROCERS

God made the wicked Grocer
For a mystery and a sign,
That men might shun the awful shops
And go to inns to dine;
Where the bacon's on the rafter
And the wine is in the wood,
And God that made good laughter
Has seen that they are good.

The evil-hearted Grocer
Would call his mother "Ma'am,"
And bow at her and bob at her,
Her aged soul to damn,
And rub his horrid hands and ask
What article was next,
Though *mortis in articulo*
Should be her proper text.

His props are not his children,
But pert lads underpaid,
Who call out "Cash!" and bang about
To work his wicked trade;
He keeps a lady in a cage
Most cruelly all day,

And makes her count and calls her "Miss"
Until she fades away.
The righteous minds of innkeepers
Induce them now and then
To crack a bottle with a friend
Or treat unmoneyed men,
But who hath seen the Grocer
Treat housemaids to his teas
Or crack a bottle of fish-sauce
Or stand a man a cheese?

He sells us sands of Araby
As sugar for cash down;
He sweeps his shop and sells the dust
The purest salt in town,
He crams with cans of poisoned meat
Poor subjects of the King,
And when they die by thousands
Why, he laughs like anything.

The wicked Grocer groces
In spirits and in wine,
Not frankly and in fellowship
As men in inns do dine;
But packed with soap and sardines
And carried off by grooms,
For to be snatched by Duchesses
And drunk in dressing-rooms.
The hell-instructed Grocer
Has a temple made of tin,
And the ruin of good innkeepers

Is loudly urged therein;
But now the sands are running out
From sugar of a sort,
The Grocer trembles; for his time,
Just like his weight, is short.

THE ROLLING ENGLISH ROAD

Before the Roman came to Rye or out to
    Severn strode,
The rolling English drunkard made the
    rolling English road.
A reeling road, a rolling road, that
    rambles round the shire,
And after him the parson ran, the sexton
    and the squire;
A merry road, a mazy road, and such as
    we did tread
The night we went to Birmingham by
    way of Beachy Head.

I knew no harm of Bonaparte and plenty
    of the Squire,
And for to fight the Frenchman I did not
    much desire;
But I did bash their baggonets because
    they came arrayed
To straighten out the crooked road an
    English drunkard made,
Where you and I went down the lane
    with ale-mugs in our hands,
The night we went to Glastonbury by

way of Goodwin Sands.
His sins they were forgiven him; or why
    do flowers run
Behind him; and the hedges all
    strengthing in the sun?
The wild thing went from left to right
    and knew not which was which,
But the wild rose was above him when
    they found him in the ditch.
God pardon us, nor harden us; we did
    not see so clear
The night we went to Bannockburn by
    way of Brighton Pier.

My friends, we will not go again or ape
    an ancient rage,
Or stretch the folly of our youth to be
    the shame of age,
But walk with clearer eyes and ears this
    path that wandereth,
And see undrugged in evening light the
    decent inn of death;
For there is good news yet to hear and
    fine things to be seen,
Before we go to Paradise by way of
    Kensal Green.

THE SONG OF QUOODLE

They haven't got no noses,
The fallen sons of Eve;
Even the smell of roses
Is not what they supposes;
But more than mind discloses
And more than men believe.

They haven't got no noses,
They cannot even tell
When door and darkness closes
The park a Jew encloses,
Where even the Law of Moses
Will let you steal a smell.

The brilliant smell of water,
The brave smell of a stone,
The smell of dew and thunder,
The old bones buried under,
Are things in which they blunder
And err, if left alone.

The wind from winter forests,
The scent of scentless flowers,
The breath of brides' adorning,

The smell of snare and warning,
The smell of Sunday morning
God gave to us for ours.

And Quoodle here discloses
All things that Quoodle can,
They haven't got no noses,
They haven't got no noses,
And goodness only knowses
The Noselessness of Man.

PIONEERS, O PIONEERS

Nebuchadnezzar the King of the Jews
Suffered from new and original views,
He crawled on his hands and knees, it's said,
With grass in his mouth and a crown on
    his head.
      With a wowtyiddly, etc.

Those in traditional paths that trod
Thought the thing was a curse from God,
But a Pioneer men always abuse
Like Nebuchadnezzar the King of the
    Jews.

Black Lord Foulon the Frenchman slew
Thought it a Futurist thing to do.
He offered them grass instead of bread.
So they stuffed him with grass when they
    cut off his head.
With a wowtyiddly, etc.

For the pride of his soul he perished
    then –
But of course it is always of Pride that
    men,

A Man in Advance of his Age accuse,
Like Nebuchadnezzar the King of the
   Jews.

Simeon Scudder of Styx, in Maine,
Thought of the thing and was at it again.
He gave good grass and water in pails
To a thousand Irishmen hammering rails.
     With a wowtyiddly, etc.
Appetites differ; and tied to a stake
He was tarred and feathered for
   Conscience' Sake.

But stoning the prophets is ancient news,
Like Nebuchadnezzar the King of the
   Jews.

THE LOGICAL VEGETARIAN

"Why shouldn't I have a purely vegetarian drink? Why shouldn't I take vegetables in their highest form, so to speak? The modest vegetarians ought obviously to stick to wine or beer, plain vegetarian drinks, instead of filling their goblets with the blood of bulls and elephants, as all conventional meat-eaters do, I suppose." – DALROY.

You will find me drinking rum,
Like a sailor in a slum,
You will find me drinking beer like a
Bavarian.
You will find me drinking gin
In the lowest kind of inn,
Because I am a rigid Vegetarian.

So I cleared the inn of wine,
And I tried to climb the sign,
And I tried to hail the constable as
"Marion."
But he said I couldn't speak,
And he bowled me to the Beak
Because I was a Happy Vegetarian.

Oh, I knew a Doctor Gluck,

And his nose it had a hook,
And his attitudes were anything but
    Aryan;
      So I gave him all the pork
      That I had, upon a fork;
Because I am myself a Vegetarian.

    I am silent in the Club,
    I am silent in the pub.,
I am silent on a bally peak in Darien;
      For I stuff away for life
      Shoving peas in with a knife,
Because I am at heart a Vegetarian.

    No more the milk of cows
    Shall pollute my private house
Than the milk of the wild mares of the
      Barbarian;
      I will stick to port and sherry,
      For they are so very, very,
So very, very, very Vegetarian.

"THE SARACEN'S HEAD"

"The Saracen's Head" looks down the lane,
Where we shall never drink wine again,
For the wicked old women who feel well-bred
Have turned to a tea-shop "The Saracen's Head."

"The Saracen's Head" out of Araby came,
King Richard riding in arms like flame,
And where he established his folk to be fed
He set up a spear – and the Saracen's Head.

But "The Saracen's Head" outlived the Kings
It thought and it thought of most horrible things,
Of Health and of Soap and of Standard Bread,
And of Saracen drinks at "The Saracen's Head."

So "The Saracen's Head" fulfils its name,
They drink no wine – a ridiculous game –
And I shall wonder until I'm dead,
How it ever came into the Saracen's Head.

THE GOOD RICH MAN

Mr Mandragon, the Millionaire, he
    wouldn't have wine or wife,
He couldn't endure complexity: he lived
    the Simple Life.
He ordered his lunch by megaphone in
    manly, simple tones,
And used all his motors for canvassing
    voters, and twenty telephones;

Besides a dandy little machine,
Cunning and neat as ever was seen,
With a hundred pulleys and cranks
    between,
Made of metal and kept quite clean,
To hoist him out of his healthful bed on
    every day of his life,
And wash him and dress him and shave
    him and brush him
        – to live the Simple Life.

Mr Mandragon was most refined and
    quietly, neatly dressed,
Say all the American newspapers that
    know refinement best;

Quiet and neat the hat and hair and the
    coat quiet and neat,
A trouser worn upon either leg, while
    boots adorn the feet;
And not, as any one would expect,
A Tiger's Skin all striped and specked,
And a Peacock Hat with the tail erect,
A scarlet tunic with sunflowers decked,
Which might have had a more marked
    effect,
And pleased the pride of a weaker man
    that yearned for wine or wife;
But Fame and the Flagon, for Mr
    Mandragon
      – obscured the Simple Life.

Mr Mandragon, the Millionaire, I am
    happy to say, is dead;
He enjoyed a quiet funeral in a
    Crematorium shed.
And he lies there fluffy and soft and grey
    and certainly quite refined;
When he might have rotted to flowers and
    fruit with Adam and all mankind,
Or been eaten by wolves athirst for blood,
Or burnt on a good tall pyre of wood,
In a towering flame, as a heathen should,
Or even sat with us here at food,
Merrily taking twopenny ale and pork
    with a pocket-knife;
But this was luxury not for one that
    went for the Simple Life.

THE SONG AGAINST SONGS

The song of the sorrow of Melisande is a
    weary song and a dreary song,
The glory of Mariana's grange had got
    into great decay,
The song of the Raven Never More has
    never been called a cheery song,
And the brightest things in Baudelaire
    are anything else but gay.

    But who will write us a riding song
    Or a hunting song or a drinking song,
    Fit for them that arose and rode
    When day and the wine were red?
    But bring me a quart of claret out,
    And I will write you a clinking song,
    A song of war and a song of wine
    And a song to wake the dead.

The song of the fury of Fragolette is a
    florid song and a torrid song,
The song of the sorrow of Tara is sung to
    a harp unstrung,
The song of the cheerful Shropshire Lad
    I consider a perfectly horrid song,

And the song of the happy Futurist is a
    song that can't be sung.

But who will write us a riding song
Or a fighting song or a drinking song,
Fit for the fathers of you and me,
That knew how to think and thrive?
But the song of Beauty and Art and
    Love
Is simply an utterly stinking song,
To double you up and drag you down
And damn your soul alive.

ME HEART

I come from Castlepatrick, and me heart
    is on me sleeve,
And any sword or pistol boy can hit it
    with me leave,
It shines there for an epaulette, as golden
    as a flame,
As naked as me ancestors, as noble as me
    name.
For I come from Castlepatrick, and me
    heart is on me sleeve,
But a lady stole it from me on St
    Gallowglass's Eve.

The folk that live in Liverpool, their
    heart is in their boots;
They go to hell like lambs, they do,
    because the hooter hoots.
Where men may not be dancin', though
    the wheels may dance all day;
And men may not be smokin'; but only
    chimneys may.
But I come from Castlepatrick, and me
    heart is on me sleeve,
But a lady stole it from me on St

Poleander's Eve.

The folk that live in black Belfast, their
    heart is in their mouth,
They see us making murders in the
    meadows of the South;
They think a plough's a rack, they do,
    and cattle-calls are creeds,
And they think we're burnin' witches
    when we're only burnin' weeds;
But I come from Castlepatrick, and me
    heart is on me sleeve;
But a lady stole it from me on St
    Barnabas's Eve.

THE SONG OF THE OAK

The Druids waved their golden knives
And danced around the Oak
When they had sacrificed a man;
But though the learned search and scan,,
No single modern person can
Entirely see the joke.
But though they cut the throats of men
They cut not down the tree,
And from the blood the saplings sprang
Of oak-woods yet to be.
    But Ivywood, Lord Ivywood,
    He rots the tree as ivy would,
    He clings and crawls as ivy would
    About the sacred tree.

King Charles he fled from Worcester fight
And hid him in an Oak;
In convent schools no man of tact
Would trace and praise his every act,
Or argue that he was in fact
A strict and sainted bloke.
But not by him the sacred woods
Have lost their fancies free,
And though he was extremely big

He did not break the tree.
   But Ivywood, Lord Ivywood,
   He breaks the tree as ivy would,
   And eats the woods as ivy would
   Between us and the sea.

Great Collingwood walked down the glade
And flung the acorns free,
That oaks might still be in the grove
As oaken as the beams above,
When the great Lover sailors love
Was kissed by Death at sea.
But though for him the oak-trees fell
To build the oaken ships,
The woodman worshipped what he smote
And honoured even the chips.
   But Ivywood, Lord Ivywood,
   He hates the tree as ivy would,
   As the dragon of the ivy would
   That has us in his grips.

THE ROAD TO ROUNDABOUT

Some say that Guy of Warwick,
The man that killed the Cow
And brake the mighty Boar alive
Beyond the Bridge at Slough;
Went up against a Loathly Worm
That wasted all the Downs,
And so the roads they twist and squirm
(If I may be allowed the term)
From the writhing of the stricken Worm
That died in seven towns
    I see no scientific proof
    That this idea is sound,
    And I should say they wound about
    To find the town of Roundabout,
    The merry town of Roundabout,
    That makes the world go round.

Some say that Robin Goodfellow,
Whose lantern lights the meads
(To steal a phrase Sir Walter Scott
In heaven no longer needs),
Such dance around the trysting-place
The moonstruck lover leads,
Which superstition I should scout

There is more faith in honest doubt
(As Tennyson has pointed out)
Than in those nasty creeds.
    But peace and righteousness (St John)
    In Roundabout can kiss,
    And since that's all that's found about
    The pleasant town of Roundabout,
    The roads they simply bound about
    To find out where it is.

Some say that when Sir Lancelot
Went forth to find the Grail,
Grey Merlin wrinkled up the roads
For hope that he should fail;
All roads led back to Lyonesse
And Camelot in the Vale,
I cannot yield assent to this
Extravagant hypothesis,
The plain, shrewd Briton will dismiss
Such rumours (*Daily Mail*).
    But in the streets of Roundabout
    Are no such factions found,
    Or theories to expound about,
    Or roll upon the ground about,
    In the happy town of Roundabout,
    That makes the world go round.

THE SONG OF THE STRANGE ASCETIC

If I had been a Heathen,
    I'd have praised the purple vine,
My slaves should dig the vineyards,
    And I would drink the wine.
But Higgins is a Heathen,
    And his slaves grow lean and grey,
That he may drink some tepid milk
    Exactly twice a day.

If I had been a Heathen,
    I'd have crowned Neœra's curls,
And filled my life with love affairs,
    My house with dancing girls;
But Higgins is a Heathen,
    And to lecture rooms is forced,
Where his aunts, who are not married,
    Demand to be divorced.

If I had been a Heathen,
    I'd have sent my armies forth,
And dragged behind my chariots
    The Chieftains of the North.
But Higgins is a Heathen,
    And he drives the dreary quill,

To lend the poor that funny cash
That makes them poorer still.

If I had been a Heathen,
I'd have piled my pyre on high,
And in a great red whirlwind
Gone roaring to the sky;
But Higgins is a Heathen,
And a richer man than I;
And they put him in an oven,
Just as if he were a pie.

Now who that runs can read it,
The riddle that I write,
Of why this poor old sinner,
Should sin without delight – ?
But I, I cannot read it
(Although I run and run),
Of them that do not have the faith,
And will not have the fun.

THE SONG OF RIGHT AND WRONG

Feast on wine or fast on water,
And your honour shall stand sure,
God Almighty's son and daughter
He the valiant, she the pure;
If an angel out of heaven
Brings you other things to drink,
Thank him for his kind attentions,
Go and pour them down the sink.

Tea is like the East he grows in,
A great yellow Mandarin
With urbanity of manner
And unconsciousness of sin;
All the women, like a harem,
At his pig-tail troop along;
And, like all the East he grows in,
He is Poison when he's strong.

Tea, although an Oriental,
Is a gentleman at least;
Cocoa is a cad and coward,
Cocoa is a vulgar beast,
Cocoa is a dull, disloyal,
Lying, crawling cad and clown,

And may very well be grateful
To the fool that takes him down.

As for all the windy waters,
They were rained like tempests down
When good drink had been dishonoured
By the tipplers of the town;
When red wine had brought red ruin
And the death-dance of our times,
Heaven sent us Soda Water
As a torment for our crimes.

WHO GOES HOME?

In the city set upon slime and loam
They cry in their parliament "Who goes
 home?
And there comes no answer in arch or
 dome,
For none in the city of graves goes home.
Yet these shall perish and understand,
For God has pity on this great land.

Men that are men again; who goes home?
Tocsin and trumpeter! Who goes home?
For there's blood on the field and blood
 on the foam
And blood on the body when Man goes home.
And a voice valedictory … Who is for
 Victory?
Who is for Liberty? Who goes home?

G K CHESTERTON

AUTOBIOGRAPHY

In *Autobiography* Chesterton describes his happy childhood, the intellectual 'doubts and morbidities' of his youth and his search for a true vocation.

He includes many anecdotes about his literary friends, Henry James, George Bernard Shaw and H G Wells.

But it is his quest for religious conviction and his conversion to Catholicism that is central to his story which he tells with great modesty, gentleness and intelligence.

CHAUCER

Chesterton expounds the 'genius of Geoffrey Chaucer' in this literary biography that explores both the writer and his time. He claims that Chaucer and his Age were 'more sane, more normal and more cheerful than writers that came after him' and the characters he portrayed have an immediate contemporary relevance.

Beautifully and sensitively written, this biography about the 'Father of English Poetry' will inform and inspire.

G K Chesterton

Criticisms and Appreciations of the Works of Charles Dickens

Written with intelligence and authority, these twenty-three essays provide an insight into the works of the literary genius of Charles Dickens.

Chesterton greatly admired Dickens as a social prophet and defender of the common man. Here, he focuses both on the style and the ideology of Dickens and provides the critical insight into his work with his characteristic perceptive generosity. Chesterton is still regarded by many as one of the most accomplished and perceptive critics of Dickens.

As much about Chesterton's strongly held beliefs as about Dickens, this volume is sure to inform and give pleasure to advocates of both writers.

George Bernard Shaw

The book traces in some detail Shaw's work as a critic (puritanical opposition to Shakespeare) and as a dramatist.

Chesterton was ideally placed to write this critical biography of the literary works and political views of George Bernard Shaw. He was a personal friend and yet an ardent opponent of Shaw's progressive socialism. The lightness of tone and the humour of his other works are equally present in his examination of Shaw. The book presents a perceptive and far from dated critique of Shaw's philosophy and politics and, through them, the emerging progressive orthodoxy of the 20th century.

The book represents an excellent introduction to Shaw's work and the spirit of the age in which it was created.

G K Chesterton

The Ball and the Cross

Evan MacIan is a passionate and fiery young Catholic. He is outraged one day by an editorial he reads in *The Atheist* and vents his anger by smashing the window of the paper's office. He then challenges the editor, Turnbull, to a duel.

The feuding men are thwarted at every turn in their attempt to find a suitable place for their fight. While the search goes on they continue their theological debate. They eventually arrive at a position of acceptance and mutual understanding before the story reaches its powerful conclusion.

The Man Who Knew Too Much

Horne Fisher is the man who knew too much. He has a brilliant mind and powers of deduction – but he always faces a moral dilemma. These eight adventures will amaze and delight as we follow Horne and his friend, Harold March, in the world of crime among eminent people.

G K Chesterton

The Man Who Was Thursday

Lucian Gregory and Gabriel Syme both dress as poets. In this disturbing fantasy, one is an Anarchist and the other is a policeman. In the surreal anarchist world they inhabit, one of them is voted onto the Anarchists' Council of Days and becomes 'Thursday'.

The Nightmare has just begun…

The Paradoxes of Mr Pond

Mr Pond was a small, neat civil servant. There was nothing remarkable about him at all – except a pointed beard. However, he tells the most fascinating stories and has the most unorthodox way of solving crimes and mysteries.

These eight short stories include the extraordinary 'The Three Horsemen of the Apocalypse' about a Marshal's plans that go tragically wrong because, paradoxically, his soldiers obey him.

G K Chesterton

The Poet and the Lunatics

Gabriel Gale is an eccentric poet. His madness is the madness of insight and he uses this gift to solve or prevent crimes committed by madmen. Chesterton ably illustrates his own premise that lunacy and sanity may just be a point of view…

The Return of Don Quixote

Michael Herne is a gentle, unassuming librarian. When he is asked to play a king in a medieval play he reluctantly agrees. After the play is over, however, strange things begin to happen. Michael refuses to change back into his everyday clothes and other actors find it impossible to return to their real character.

Set in the early 20th Century, this is the intriguing story of the rise of a new Don Quixote who introduces a medieval government into the world of big business.

Made in the USA
Monee, IL
07 July 2026